SOUTH DEVON COLLEGE LIBRARY

D0188258

SOUTH DEVON COLL. LIB.	
90456	337.142 094
ACC	CLASS 36

The European Union

Union

Political, Social, and Economic Cooperation

THE
EUROPEAN UNION

POLITICAL, SOCIAL, AND ECONOMIC COOPERATION

The European Union

Political, Social, and Economic Cooperation

AUSTRIA

by
Jeanine Sanna

Mason Crest Publishers
Philadelphia

Mason Crest Publishers Inc.
370 Reed Road, Broomall, Pennsylvania 19008
(866) MCP-BOOK (toll free)
www.masoncrest.com

Copyright © 2006 by Mason Crest Publishers. All rights reserved. No part of this publication may be reproduced or transmitted in any form or by any means, electronic or mechanical, including photocopying, recording, taping, or any information storage and retrieval system, without permission from the publisher.

First printing
1 2 3 4 5 6 7 8 9 10

Library of Congress Cataloging-in-Publication Data

Sanna, Jeanine.
  Austria / by Jeanine Sanna.
     p. cm.—(European Union : political, social, and economic cooperation)
  Includes index.
    ISBN 1-4222-0039-6
    ISBN 1-4222-0038-8 (series)
  1. European Union—Austria—Juvenile literature. 2. Austria–Juvenile literature. I. Title. II. European Union (Series) (Philadelphia, Pa.)
  DB17.S26 2006
   —dc22
                              2005012950

Produced by Harding House Publishing Service, Inc.
www.hardinghousepages.com
Interior design by Benjamin Stewart.
Cover design by MK Bassett-Harvey.
Printed in the Hashemite Kingdom of Jordan.

CONTENTS

THE EUROPEAN UNION

AUSTRIA

European Union Member since 1995

Grnünd

Krems

Wels
Linz
St. Pölten

Steyr

Baden
Vienna

Salzburg
Wiener
Neustadt
Eisenstadt

Bregenz

Kufstein

Bischofshofen

Feldkirch
Innsbruck
Leoben
Bruck

Landeck

Badgastein
Graz

Lienz

Villach
Klagenfurt

INTRODUCTION

Sixty years ago, Europe lay scarred from the battles of the Second World War. During the next several years, a plan began to take shape that would unite the countries of the European continent so that future wars would be inconceivable. On May 9, 1950, French Foreign Minister Robert Schuman issued a declaration calling on France, Germany, and other European countries to pool together their coal and steel production as "the first concrete foundation of a European federation." "Europe Day" is celebrated each year on May 9 to commemorate the beginning of the European Union (EU).

The EU consists of twenty-five countries, spanning the continent from Ireland in the west to the border of Russia in the east. Eight of the ten most recently admitted EU member states are former communist regimes that were behind the Iron Curtain for most of the latter half of the twentieth century.

Any European country with a democratic government, a functioning market economy, respect for fundamental rights, and a government capable of implementing EU laws and policies may apply for membership. Bulgaria and Romania are set to join the EU in 2007. Croatia and Turkey have also embarked on the road to EU membership.

While the EU began as an idea to ensure peace in Europe through interconnected economies, it has evolved into so much more today:

- Citizens can travel freely throughout most of the EU without carrying a passport and without stopping for border checks.

- EU citizens can live, work, study, and retire in another EU country if they wish.

- The euro, the single currency accepted throughout twelve of the EU countries (with more to come), is one of the EU's most tangible achievements, facilitating commerce and making possible a single financial market that benefits both individuals and businesses.

- The EU ensures cooperation in the fight against cross-border crime and terrorism.

- The EU is spearheading world efforts to preserve the environment.

- As the world's largest trading bloc, the EU uses its influence to promote fair rules for world trade, ensuring that globalization also benefits the poorest countries.

- The EU is already the world's largest donor of humanitarian aid and development assistance, providing 55 percent of global official development assistance to developing countries in 2004.

The EU is neither a nation intended to replace existing nations, nor an international organization. The EU is unique—its member countries have established common institutions to which they delegate some of their sovereignty so that decisions on matters of joint interest can be made democratically at the European level.

Europe is a continent with many different traditions and languages, but with shared values such as democracy, freedom, and social justice, cherished values well known to North Americans. Indeed, the EU motto is "United in Diversity."

Enjoy your reading. Take advantage of this chance to learn more about Europe and the EU!

Ambassador John Bruton,
Head of Delegation of the European Commission, Washington, D.C.

Kamacher mountainside in Austria.

THE LANDSCAPE

Referred to as the East-West hub of Europe since it connects both sides of the continent, Austria is known for its long history of music. Perhaps its biggest claim to fame is the fact that it is the birthplace of well-known composer Wolfgang Amadeus Mozart. This landlocked country was once the center of the Austro-Hungarian Empire. Now, its food, leisure activities, and geography make it a popular vacation spot.

The Geography

Austria is a relatively small country, covering about 32,274 square miles (83,858 square kilometers). This may seem large, but consider the fact that the whole country is about the size of Maine. Austria is completely surrounded by land; it shares borders with eight different countries: Switzerland, Liechtenstein, Germany, Czech Republic, Slovakia, Hungary, Slovenia, and Italy.

A Country Covered with Mountains

Austria is one of the most mountainous countries in the world, with more than 80 percent of its surface covered with mountain ranges. It has an average elevation of 3,000 feet (910 meters). The highest mountain in the country is the Grossglockner, which is about 12,500 feet tall (3,797 meters). This is taller than four Empire State buildings stacked on each other! Wide valleys intersect these peaks, creating many different geographic areas.

The first of these is the Alps, famous for their skiing. The Alpine region includes mountains from the west to the south. This famous mountain range has a high amount of precipitation, along with short summers and long winters. In the valleys, the air is warm and dry. From twenty to forty days a year these valleys experience a dry wind called *föhn*. This is most common in the spring and fall and can be dangerous, since the force of

Quick Facts: The Geography of Austria

Location: central Europe, north of Italy and Slovenia
Area: (slightly smaller than the state of Maine)
total: 32,382 square miles (83,870 sq. km.)
land: 31,832 square miles (82,444 sq. km.)
water: 551 square miles (1,426 sq. km.)
Borders: Czech Republic 225 miles (362 km.), Germany 487 miles (784 km.), Hungary 227 miles (366 km.), Italy 267 miles (430 km.), Liechtenstein 22 miles (35 km.), Slovakia 57 miles (91 km.), Slovenia 205 miles (330 km.), Switzerland 110 miles (164 km.)
Climate: temperate; continental, cloudy; cold winters with frequent rain and some snow in the lowlands and snow in the mountains; moderate summers with occasional showers
Terrain: west and south mostly mountains (Alps); east and north flat or gently sloping
Elevation extremes:
lowest point: Neusiedler See—377 feet (115 meters)
highest point: Grossglockner—12,461 feet (3,798 meters)
Natural hazards: landslides, avalanches, earthquakes

Source: www.cia.gov, 2005.

The Alps behind the town of Innsbruck

the wind can cause large rocks to fall off the faces of the mountains, leading to avalanches. The wind is so dry that it also leads to a high probability of fires. The winters in this area are long and the summers short.

The second geographic region is in southeast Austria, which contains sheltered valleys that are quite a bit warmer than their Alpine counterparts. This leads to an earlier spring, but winter is still just as harsh as in the mountains—about 4°F (−15°C). The weather here is characterized by frequent heavy thunderstorms.

To the northeast and east lie the respective Vienna and Danube basins, Austria's driest areas.

CHAPTER ONE—THE LANDSCAPE

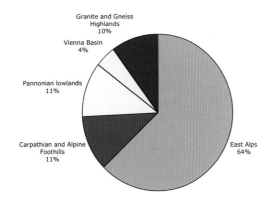

Geographic Composition of Austria

Granite and Gneiss Highlands 10%

Vienna Basin 4%

Pannonian lowlands 11%

Carpathian and Alpine Foothills 11%

East Alps 64%

Because the air is so dry, they rarely receive a deep snowfall, but what snow there is can last for weeks during the cold winters. The summers are warm, but not hot, with an average of about 68°F (20°C). If you don't like cool weather, Austria is not the country for you!

BODIES OF WATER

While it has many rivers and lakes, Austria's most important body of water is the Danube River, which is 217.4 miles (350 kilometers) long. This waterway **bisects** the northern section of the country as it flows from west to east. The Danube is an important means of transportation and has been the focus of songs and stories throughout history, most notably the "Blue Danube Waltz" by Johann Strauss.

Austria has many lakes within its borders. One of these is Lake Neusiedl, a bird haven home to many unique species. Another is Lake Langbathsee, which is surrounded by scenery so picturesque that in prior times, Emperor Franz Josef built a summer lodge here. The Attersee is the largest lake in Austria, followed by the Traunsee. These large, deep lakes are cooler than the rest, and their water is of a better quality for drinking.

VEGETATION

Austria is one of Europe's most heavily wooded countries, and because of its varied climate, it has many types of plants. The vegetation varies from **deciduous** forests, to mixed forests with trees like beech and fir.

At the higher altitudes, one can see trees such as fir, larch, and pine. The northern edge of the Alps is mostly grassland, while to the east are many plants found only on the **salt steppes** east of Lake Neusiedl.

Many types of plants grow only on the mountains. Although they only bloom for a short time, the sight of them is beautiful. These include such plants as edelweiss, gentians, primroses, and monkshoods.

Austrians have set aside 3 percent of their country for parks. These preserves highlight unique and endangered plants that cannot be found anywhere else. The nature parks include rain forests, as well as virgin forests that have grown for thousands of years, untouched by human activity.

Austria's lakes, mountains, and forests

Mountain goats grazing

WILDLIFE

The animals that live in Austria are more or less native to all of Europe. These include deer, **marmot**, fox, badger, and **martin**. The Alpine regions have different species of wildlife, such as the chamois—which is similar to a cross between a goat and an antelope—the groundhog, eagle, and mountain jackdaw.

Austria is also home to many endangered species, such as grizzly bears and lynx. The golden eagle and the wood grouse are protected, while not yet endangered. Austria has also helped some endangered species return. For example, the **ibex** and the wild boar have both been reintroduced to the wild, and their populations are gradually increasing.

Austria's rich natural resources have played their part in the land's history. Its land and its long historical heritage have helped shape the modern nation and its government.

One of Austria's many historical buildings

2 CHAPTER

AUSTRIA'S HISTORY AND GOVERNMENT

Austria has been populated for thousands of years; evidence has been found that shows humans have lived in that area since the Paleolithic Age (about 80,000 to 10,000 BCE). In 1991, the mummy of a man dating back to the Stone Age was found in the ice of the Alps, almost perfectly preserved.

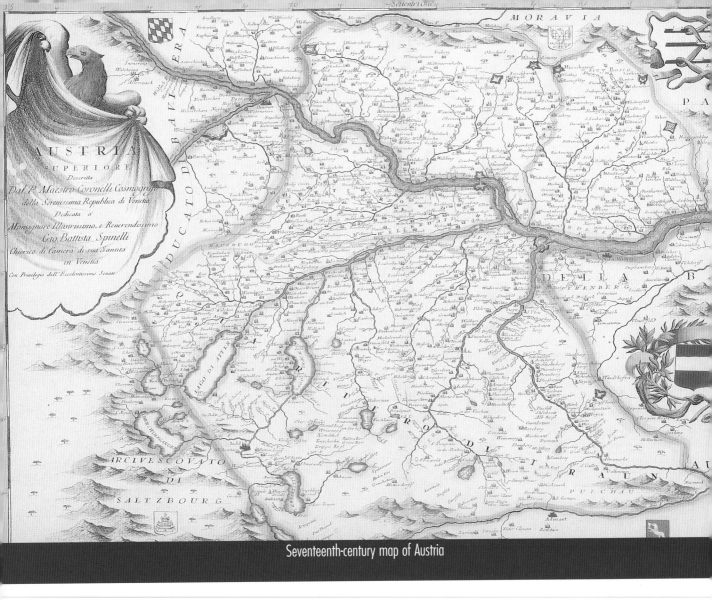

Seventeenth-century map of Austria

Later on, from about 800 to 400 BCE, many ***Celtic*** tribes inhabited Austria, trading with others from all over Europe. This was a period when many groups invaded the land, partly because of the availability and convenience of the Danube River. These tribes included the Celts, as well as the Romans and others.

THE ROMAN EMPIRE

The Romans founded Vienna, now the capital of Austria. They settled many other towns as well and in the second century CE brought about the spread of Christianity to the region.

When the Roman Empire lost power around 470 CE, the Roman culture that had **permeated** the area disappeared. From this point on, Austria was prey to many wandering tribes and armies. Then, in the eighth century, Charlemagne established the territory as part of his Holy Roman Empire. This lasted until his death in 907, after which **anarchy** reigned until Otto the Great conquered the area in 955.

THE BABENBERG DYNASTY

After this era, which lasted for around twenty years, a new family took control. These were the Babenbergs, whose rule lasted for more than three centuries. They were the ones who gave the region its name: *Österreich* or Austria.

In the thirteenth century, however, the emperor of the Holy Roman Empire invaded Austria. He refused to recognize the rule of the Babenberg king, and both sides fought. King Ottokar was killed on the battlefield, and Emperor Rudolf von Hapsburg took control, starting a dynasty that would last more than six hundred years.

DATING SYSTEMS AND THEIR MEANING

You might be accustomed to seeing dates expressed with the abbreviations BC or AD, as in the year 1000 BC or the year AD 1900. For centuries, this dating system has been the most common in the Western world. However, since BC and AD are based on Christianity (BC stands for Before Christ and AD stands for *anno Domini*, Latin for "in the year of our Lord"), many people now prefer to use abbreviations that people from all religions can be comfortable using. The abbreviations BCE (meaning Before Common Era) and CE (meaning Common Era) mark time in the same way (for example, 1000 BC is the same year as 1000 BCE, and AD 1900 is the same year as 1900 CE), but BCE and CE do not have the same religious overtones as BC and AD.

HAPSBURG RULE

The Hapsburgs expanded their territory; over time, the family controlled the land in Bohemia, Spain, and Hungary, as well as Austria. The empire was forced to divide because of its great size—eventually, there were two branches, one controlling the area around Austria and Germany, the other in charge of Spain and Holland. However, this power would not last forever.

While the Hapsburg rulers were busy expanding their territory, they were ignoring the potential threat of the Ottomans. This group gained in power, until in 1453, they took control of Constantinople, the capital of the Holy Roman Empire. Twice they were able to invade as far as Vienna, but both times they met fierce resistance at the city limits. Finally, under Prince Eugene of Savoy, the army was able to rid the country of the Turks and take back their territory.

PROTESTANTISM

Although seemingly peaceful now, the empire still had problems to face. As **economies** based on **currency** spread, the importance of Austrian trade routes decreased. Because of economic and political instability, the **Protestant Revolution** spread rapidly in Austria. The Hapsburgs tried to undo the results of this spread of Protestantism through the Counter Revolution. This alliance between the Austrian government and the Catholic Church continued throughout the rule of the Hapsburg dynasty.

At first, it was impossible to keep the Protestants from practicing their religion, and so the rulers of Austria opted for a practice of **toleration**. However, under Ferdinand II, the strong feelings against Protestants led to the Thirty Years' War (1618–1648). After the war ended with the Peace of Westphalia, the Hapsburg lands became their own empire, separate from the Holy Roman Empire, which gradually lost power and faded into the background.

In 1700, the last Spanish Hapsburg died. This caused many clashes between governments as many countries tried to win control of Spain. Austria lost this War of Spanish **Succession**, but it was able to keep control of its territories in Italy and the Netherlands.

At this time, the monarchy was not absolute. In other words, it left many rights to the provinces, such as taxation. However, other powers still rested in the hands of the emperor, including the **repression** of free speech and worship.

MARIA THERESA— THE FIRST QUEEN OF AUSTRIA

In 1740, Emperor Karl VI died without any male heirs. Thus, out of necessity, the crown passed to his daughter, Maria Theresa. The new empress was forced to prove herself in more than one war as she fought off those like the Prussian king Fredrich II who yearned after her lands. Throughout both the Silesian War (1740–1748) and the Seven Years' War (1756–1763), she managed to keep her territory together. The only

Maria Theresa

province she lost was Silesia, which she gave up to Prussia.

Maria Theresa's husband was later elected emperor of the Holy Roman Empire. However, he was never as successful as the strong woman he married. She and her son Joseph II put into place many reforms that are still important today, including the abolishment of **serfdom** and the **secularization** of monasteries and other church lands.

THE FRENCH REVOLUTION BRINGS NEW IDEAS

This peaceful age of monarchs lasted until the 1790s when the French Revolution brought ideas of equality and democracy to Austria. Threatened by these new ideals, Emperor Franz II, the grandson of Maria Theresa and the nephew of the French queen Marie Antoinette (who was beheaded during the revolution), took action. He joined a **coalition** against France. This might have seemed like a good idea at the time, but Austria later suffered great losses under the invasion of Napoleon Bonaparte.

The two countries became involved in a power struggle. Napoleon crowned himself emperor of France in 1804, and Franz followed his example by creating the Empire of Austria. In 1806, the Holy Roman Empire dissolved because of the Confederation of the Rhine—a group of fifteen German states who joined with France. Therefore, Franz was forced to give up his crown. From then on Napoleon was able to inflict heavy losses on Austria. He even went so far as to conquer Vienna twice. However, he, like all other men, was not indestructible. He was finally defeated at Waterloo and was exiled to the Island of Saint Helen's, where he died in 1821. The old order of monarchies was restored in Europe.

THE MONARCHY WEAKENS

Early in 1848, the idea of freedom for the middle classes again reached Austria from France. This time the people asked for **freedom of the press** as well as a **constitution**. The hated **police system** of the time was swept away, but the remainder of the revolution was stopped. Emperor Franz Joseph I put into place a system that left no room for anything except the absolute right of a monarch to rule.

Because of his rule and policy of neutrality, especially in the Crimean War (1854–1856), Austria found itself without friends or allies when it was attacked by Sardinia. Three years later, Austria was forced to give up its territory of Lombardy. With the October Diploma and the February Edict, the country also put in place a **parliament**.

The government was weakening, and reorganization was needed. In 1867, a compromise was reached that put in place a dual state: the Austro-Hungarian Empire. A cultural minority ruled the people, making other groups, especially the Slavs, unhappy.

Around this time, two political parties—the Social Democratic Party and the Christian Social Party—emerged. Both demanded civil rights for the

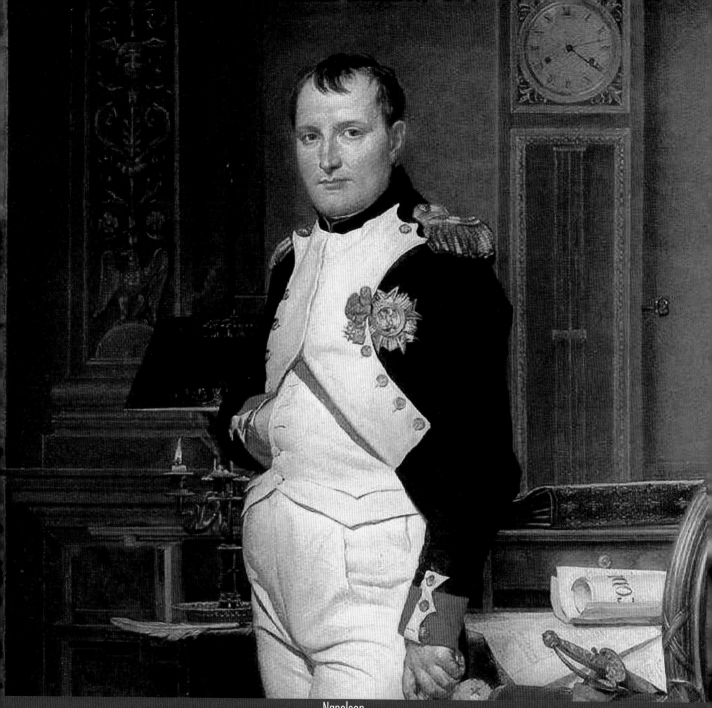
Napoleon

Modern Austria echoes the long-ago land.

people and were able to let their voices be heard in Austria's first general election in 1907. **Anti-Semitism** also spread at this time as many poor Jews moved to Austria from the eastern provinces of the empire. Despite these setbacks, some aspects of the culture flourished, and Vienna became a major center of the arts.

Austria was relatively peaceful from this time until the beginning of World War I. It had learned from its previous mistakes and formed alliances with other countries, including the German Empire and Italy, in the Triple Alliance. However, feelings of **nationalism** were growing, causing tensions to rise. People also demanded better pay and

working conditions, setting the stage for World War I to begin.

WORLD WAR

On June 28, 1914, Archduke Franz Ferdinand was assassinated. He was the heir to the Austria throne, and his murder by a member of a nationalist group caused the tensions that had been building for years to flare into a full-fledged war.

The first three years of fighting were futile; none of the European nations emerged with a clear lead. The entrance of the United States into World War I in 1917 helped tip the scales against the Central Powers (Austria-Hungary, the German Empire, and Turkey). After the war ended, the Austro-Hungarian Empire dissolved into small nation states, which later formed the Republic of Austria.

In 1919, at the end of the war, the Treaty of Saint-Germain established fixed borders for Austria. It also made sure that the new country was forbidden to form any alliances with Germany. In the end, Austria was a small country of about 7 million people, more than a third of who lived in Vienna. While the empire had been self-sufficient, Austria now was forced to look elsewhere for raw materials, food, and markets for its goods. Because of this, the economy crashed and a period of starvation ensued. Inflation set in, which was only stopped when the League of Nations (a **precursor** to the United Nations) stepped in and helped.

SOCIALISM IN AUSTRIA

The postwar country's political views swerved as far from monarchy as is possible. Two **socialist** factions, the "Red," who were more moderate, and the "Black," who believed that the clergy should have more power, headed the new socialist views. Conflict escalated between the two groups when the Black won the 1921 election, and riots raged in the streets of Vienna. In the end, two private **militias** both posed a threat to the government. Eventually, the National Socialist Party (the Black) gained popularity, partly because of the increase in anti-Semitism.

A new chancellor, Engelbert Dollfus, came into power in 1932. He was against National Socialism; however, he believed in **fascism**. Because of this, he quickly became involved with Mussolini, the Italian fascist leader of the time. Because he was so suppressive of the socialists, a revolt occurred in 1934, but the army soon put it down. After this demonstration, all political parties were banned, and a **totalitarian** state was put into place. Dollfus was assassinated in 1934.

At this time, German influence, led by Adolph Hitler, increased in Austria. The new chancellor, Kurt von Schuschnigg, appointed the National Socialists to government posts. Finally, Hitler forced Schuschnigg to resign, and Austria was occupied by German troops in 1938.

After World War II, when Germany was **vanquished**, Austria regained its freedom when the Allies decided to reestablish Austria as an independent nation in 1943. In 1945, it was taken over by Soviet and American troops and a **provisional government** was set in place. The original constitution was restored with one major revision: the country was now divided into separate occupation zones, each controlled by a different Allied power.

RECONSTRUCTION

Now began the job of reconstructing the economy and the government. However, recovery didn't go as fast as was expected because of the decline of trade between the two halves of Europe. Eastern Europe remained communist with tension between it and the democratic Western Europe. Finally, in 1955, a formal treaty between France, Great Britain, the United States, the USSR (the Soviets), and Austria put the Austrian government back in the hands of its native citizens. There was a heavy price, though: Austria had to pay **reparations** to the USSR, as well as promise to remain neutral in all future conflicts and to never purchase or develop weapons of mass destruction. After this treaty was passed, Austria was allowed into the United Nations.

By the 1960s, Austria was back on its feet. The country had joined the European Free Trade Association in 1959, allowing it to trade without

Modern Austria

Downtown modern Salzburg

having to pay tariffs to the other European nations. The balance of power between the liberals and the conservatives was about equal, with both the People's Party and the Socialists maintaining control at various times.

MODERN GOVERNMENT

In 1983, the Socialist government fell, and it joined forces with the *radical* Freedom Party. Three years later, Kurt Waldheim was elected president, despite rumors he had been involved in *atrocities* as a German officer during World War II. His election caused controversy throughout the world.

By the late 1980s, Austria had become more *capitalist* as it started to *privatize* some state-owned industries. In 1995, it entered the European Union (EU).

Today, Austria's government has three main parties: the People's Party, the Social Democrats, and the Freedom Party, which is far *right* and radical. In 2000, the People's Party and Freedom Party joined together so that a stable government could be formed, but this led to Austria being criticized by the rest of the EU because of the radical Freedom Party's involvement in the government. The Freedom Party members argued among themselves, leading to a collapse of the government. As of today, the People's and Freedom parties have again joined, regardless of the fact that their alliance failed once before.

Despite the political upheaval that Austria has faced over the years, its economy has managed to thrive.

3 THE ECONOMY

After World War II, the government took control of many of Austria's industries to prevent them from coming under the control of the USSR for the payment of war reparations. Because of this, for a long time the government had a large role in the economy. In the past twenty years, however, the country has started to privatize businesses. This process has been mainly successful, although the government still owns some industries and services.

Despite being in the middle of changing hands, Austria's economy is very strong for various reasons. One of these is that now, as throughout history, Austria serves as a hub between many countries. Goods flow through the country, especially those used in fuels like oil and natural gas.

Not only goods but people as well gather in Austria. The country has been the site of countless treaty meetings and international conferences. Each time this happens, business is brought into the country from international sources, helping the economy.

Austria places a great influence on aiding the poor and less fortunate and helps them improve their lot in life. This is done through **income transfers**, such as welfare.

QUICK FACTS: THE ECONOMY OF AUSTRIA

Gross Domestic Product (GDP): $245.3 billion (2004 est.)

GDP per capita: $30,000

Industries: construction, machinery, vehicles and parts, food, chemicals, lumber and wood processing, paper and paperboard, communications equipment, tourism

Agriculture: grains, potatoes, sugar beets, wine, fruit; dairy products, cattle, pigs, poultry; lumber

Export commodities: machinery and equipment, motor vehicles and parts, paper and paperboard, metal goods, chemicals, iron and steel; textiles, foodstuffs

Export partners: Germany 35%, Italy 9%, France 5%, Hungary 4%, Switzerland 5%, U.S. 5%

Import commodities: machinery and equipment, motor vehicles, chemicals, metal goods, oil and oil products, foodstuffs

Import partners: Germany 42%, Italy 7%, France 5%, Hungary 4%, U.S. 6%, Switzerland 3%

Currency: euro

Currency exchange rate: U.S.$1 = €.78 (May 2, 2005)

Note: All figures are from 2004 unless noted.
Source: www.cia.gov, 2004.

INDUSTRIES

Austria is highly industrialized and makes such goods as vehicle engines, as well as other electronic parts, like airbag chips and braking systems, for cars. However, the country is also known for the high percentage of its people who are employed by smaller companies. For example, many are involved in the craft-making industry. Austria is famous for handmade items like jewelry, ceramics, and blown glass. Tourism also contributes to the country's **Gross Domestic Product (GDP)**, as people from all over the world visit this beautiful country.

A busy city street

While much of the economy consists of smaller businesses, there are some large industries like iron and steel processing plants, as well as a large chemical manufacturing business. Other goods that are manufactured in Austria are lumber and processed wood, such as paper, computers and other communication equipment, and machinery.

Part of the reason that Austria is so prosperous is the abundance of raw materials from which the country can draw. The land is rich with deposits of iron and other important minerals buried deep below the earth's surface. Austria also has its own sources of oil and natural gas. As scientists work to end the world's dependence on oil, Austria is

now generating **hydroelectric** power and is now the country that supplies the most to other members of the EU.

IMPORTS AND EXPORTS

Altogether, Austria trades with over 150 countries; the member countries in the EU account for more than two-thirds of all exports. Most of these goods go to Germany, Italy, France, Switzerland, and Great Britain. The United States also trades with Austria. The country exports such things as machinery, motor vehicles, paper, chemicals, iron, fabrics, and food.

In return for these goods, Austria receives many others. These include chemicals, metal goods, oil, and mechanical equipment. Many of the goods are the same as those they import, and while this might seem **redundant**, there is a reason. When a country produces a good, they are also using up resources that might have been used in making different goods. Most of the time countries manufacture the goods with the least **opportunity costs**; this allows them to make as many things as possible. However, sometimes another country can make the same good cheaper; in other words, it has a **comparative advantage**. In that case, the two countries will trade.

AUSTRIAN AGRICULTURE

About 18 percent of Austria is farmland. While this may not seem like a lot, about 5 percent of all people work in agriculture (compare this to the 1 percent of Americans who farm). The country also has about 20,000 **organic** farms, making it one of the most important countries in Europe for this type of agriculture.

Many foodstuffs are produced in Austria, including such things as grains, potatoes, and fruit. The country also has many dairy products as well as cattle, pigs, and poultry. Some of the fresh foods are made into other products such as wine.

TRANSPORTATION

Austria has an efficient transportation system, with roads, waterways, airlines, and railroads all providing ways to get from one place to another. Vienna in particular has many ways to get around, including streetcars, subways, buses, and commuter trains. This transportation network not only serves to connect Austria's thriving economy; it also connects its people and culture.

Visitors to one of Austria's museums

CHAPTER 4 — AUSTRIA'S PEOPLE AND CULTURE

Austria is home to over 8.2 million people. Its citizens come from all over Eastern Europe, including Croatia, Slovakia, Hungary, Slovenia, Romania, and Czech Republic. However, the Ethnic Groups Act of 1976 only recognizes

Salzburg's many churches reflect Austria's religious heritage.

those ethnic groups that have lived in Austria for more than three geneations and who are Austrian citizens. These recognized ethnic groups are scattered throughout Austria. In Burgenland are the Croatians and Hungarians. The Slovenians have made their home in the Gail, Rosen, and Jaun valleys in the south, while the Czechs and Slovaks live in Vienna and southern Austria.

No matter what the cultural background of Austrian citizens, they have one thing that ties most of them together: a common language. Ninety-eight percent of the population speaks German.

RELIGION

In Austria, there is a law that states everyone over fourteen is allowed to choose their own religion. However, the majority (about 78 percent) is Catholic. This stems from the old Hapsburg dynasty, which was a Catholic power. During the Hapsburg reign, the government persecuted all non-Catholics. It was not until 1867 that a policy of religious tolerance was put into place, and while everyone is now free to make their own decisions regarding religion, many cling to their old faith.

In 1908, the Austro-Hungarian Empire took control of Bosnia Herzegovina, with its large percentage of Muslims in the population. Because of this, Austria was the first in Europe to officially recognize the Muslim faith. Today, other religious minorities include Protestants, Buddhists, Mormons, Jews, and Greek-Orthodox.

Catholics are known for their religious education, but in Austria they are not the only providers of religious schools. Many smaller churches and other religious groups also offer education based on their faith. While in the United States these are private schools and paid for through tuition from the families who attend, in Austria all education—including religious education—is paid for by the state.

EDUCATION

The Austrian school system has been developing since Maria Theresa put forth the "General School Regulations," a set of guidelines for schools in 1774. Now all students must attend at least nine years of schooling, from the time they are six until age fourteen. If, after that, teens wish to drop out of school, they can attend a polytechnic course that will prepare them for a job.

School starts at the elementary level, which lasts for four years. After that, students attend secondary school. Once this level is completed, there are many choices teens and their families can make. One school is the *allgemein bildende höhere Sculen*, which is mostly general education, much like an American high school. Austrian students, however, can either focus on the arts or sciences. Vocational schools are another option, one that provides practical job training to students. After completing either of these types of course, students are issued a certificate much like a high school diploma, that allows the bearer to apply to a university.

Austrian education is nationally regulated, and all schools must hold to the same standards. However, some educators are working toward letting school districts have more freedom in creating their students' curriculum. All schools are free of charge, as are textbooks and transportation to and from school.

QUICK FACTS: THE PEOPLE OF AUSTRIA

Population: 8,174,762 (July 2004 est.)

Ethnic groups: Germans 88.5%, indigenous minorities (includes Croatians, Slovenes, Hungarians, Czechs, Slovaks, Roma) 1.5%, recent immigrant groups (includes Turks, Bosnians, Serbians, Croatians) 10%

Age structure:
  0-14 years: 15.9%
  15-64 years: 68.1%
  65 years and above: 16%

Population growth rate: 0.14%

Birth rate: 8.9 births/1,000 pop.

Death rate: 9.56 deaths/1,000 pop.

Migration rate: 2 migrants/1,000 pop.

Infant mortality rate: 4.68 deaths/1,000 live births

Life expectancy at birth:
  Total population: 78.87 years
  Male: 76 years
  Female: 81.89 years

Total fertility rate: 1.35 children born/woman

Religions: Roman Catholic 73.6%, Protestant 4.7%, Muslim 4.2%, other 0.1%, none 17.4%

Languages: German (official nationwide), Slovene (official in Carinthia), Croatian and Hungarian (official in Burgenland)

Literacy rate: 98%

Note: All figures are from 2004 unless otherwise noted.
Source: www.cia.gov, 2005.

FOOD

Reflecting the diverse population, Austrian food features a great variety of specialties, many of which are known throughout the world. Among these delicacies is *Weiner Schnitzel*, which is fried, breaded veal. Other popular Austrian dishes include *strudels* (or pies) and *Kaiserschmarrn*, a type of potato salad.

MUSIC AND LITERATURE

Austria is very proud of the fact that it is the birthplace of Wolfgang Amadeus Mozart, the prolific composer who wrote hundreds of songs. Many other famous composers called Austria home as well, including Ludwig van Beethoven, Johannes Brahms, Joseph Haydn, Franz Schubert, Johann Strauss Sr. and Johann Strauss Jr. Not all of Austria's musicians lived hundreds of years ago; the country is also home to famous modern groups like Flaco and DJ Ötzi.

Austria has given birth to many famous literary figures as well. One such author, Joseph Roth, became well known for his portrayal of the downfall of the Hapsburg Empire. One of his novels, *Savoy Hotel*, tells of life in a hotel and shows it as a haven for people in trouble who are looking to escape.

Mozart's house

A Salzburg snack bar

Another Austrian author is Felix Salten. While the name may not sound familiar, he is the man behind the story *Bambi*, which was later turned into an animated movie by Walt Disney. Other literary figures include Ferdinand Raimond, Ingeborg Bachmann, and Peter Handke.

ARTS AND ARCHITECTURE

While many of the Austrian painters are less well known than some of the other artists of similar time periods, the country is still home to much artistic talent. One such artist is Gustav Klimt. Klimt's work dates from the late nineteenth century and is characterized by intensive colors and symbolism, as well as sometimes using a gold background. His work was very controversial at the time because of its **erotic** elements, but he has become very popular with Austrians today. Other Austrian painters include Egon Schiele (1890–1918), Oskar Kokoschka (1886–1980), and Friedensreich Hundertwasser (1928–2000).

Austrian architecture, especially in the city of Vienna, represents a diversity of time periods and styles. The country is a hodgepodge of different buildings, from the **baroque** to the **avant-garde** styles.

FESTIVALS AND EVENTS

Austria celebrates many festivals and events throughout the year, many of which are smaller, regional activities. Many of these center around music, with many festivals celebrating Austria's many composers. These provide a time to listen to and perform the music of such famous musicians as Mozart, Beethoven, and Strauss.

Austria also has many religious holidays, like Epiphany, Easter, St. Nicolas Day, and Christmas. Austrians celebrate All Souls Day on November 1 as a time to honor the dead. Children are given gifts and food while the souls are told that a tolling bell allows them to leave this earth.

These festivities are celebrated across Austria, but particularly in the cities, where most Austrians make their homes.

Three of the Most Famous Austrians

Sigmund Freud, the father of psychoanalysis
Wolfgang Puck, celebrity chef
Arnold Schwarzenegger, actor and governor of California

Busy Salzburg street

5 CHAPTER THE CITIES

While there are many small villages and hamlets in Austria, most of the population lives in larger cities. Sixty-eight percent of people live in urban areas, while the others are spread out throughout the country. Family size in urban areas, as well as the rest of Austria, is relatively small, with most families only having one or two children.

These cities are of varied size and population, the largest being Vienna, which is home to more than 2 million inhabitants. Other major cities include Graz, Innsbruck, and Salzburg.

VIENNA: THE CAPITAL OF AUSTRIA

The most populated city in Austria, Vienna is steeped in history. This city is where the former Hapsburg Empire was centered, and many historical buildings from this time can still be seen. Visitors can visit St. Stephan's Cathedral, which continues to reflect the glory and extravagance of the Baroque era. There is also The Ring, an avenue around the old capitol buildings and palaces that provides a glimpse of historic Austria.

There are many events that go on in Vienna, including an annual marathon, numerous operas and other musical events, and a Lifeball that is organized every year as an AIDS awareness and fundraising event. At the end of April, a festival is set up in the museum quarter that lasts until September. Here one can see various exhibits, listen to music, and drink the refreshments that are served in the courtyard between the museums.

GRAZ

Situated on the edge of the Alps, this ancient city was built by the Romans and started as a small castle. As time passed, the city grew, and now many different types and eras of architecture can be seen there, including the Renaissance-style Country House, one of Graz's most well-known

buildings. The first Austrian university was built in Graz in 1586, paving the way for the city's tradition of supporting education. Today, the city has at least seven colleges, including medical and art schools.

This city has something for everyone. Graz hosts a jazz festival each summer as well as various film festivals. There are also many sights to see, including the ruin of Goesting Castle. This former chateau was struck by lightning, but it is now one of the most popular spots to visit in the city.

INNSBRUCK

The name of this city comes from an old bridge that runs over a stream to the town inn, formerly in the center of town. The city's coat of arms portrays this bridge, leading to its name.

Innsbruck is a very athletic city; almost any physical activity that one can imagine goes on here— rock climbing, sky diving, mountain biking, and

Innsbruck from the Alps

skateboarding, to name a few. Innsbruck, like the rest of Austria, also places a high emphasis on music and the arts and is home to the National Theatre.

A restaurant terrace in downtown Salzburg

SALZBURG

Salzburg is the birthplace of the musician Mozart. Because of this, many festivals celebrating his music take place throughout the year. The city is very proud of its most famous resident, and visitors can still see the house where this child prodigy was born.

As well as being home to one of the most well-known composers of all time, Salzburg is also where the musical *The Sound of Music* takes place. What some don't know is that the von Trapp family really existed and lived in Salzburg in the 1930s. Mr. von Trapp hired a former nun as a nanny for his children, who then persuaded the family to turn their love of singing together into a moneymaking venture in which they were paid for performing. Once Hitler came into power, the family fled to America, leaving everything they owned behind them. Eventually, they made their fortune in the United States, where they became famous and toured until 1956.

These cities form Austria's backbone, the ancient skeleton on which its culture and economy are built. Being a part of the EU, however, has added new flesh to Austria, bringing fresh life to its culture, its economy, and its cities.

The EU flag

6 THE FORMATION OF THE EUROPEAN UNION

The EU is an economic and political confederation of twenty-five European nations. Member countries abide by common foreign and security policies and cooperate on judicial and domestic affairs. The confederation, however, does not replace existing states or governments. Each of the twenty-five member states is *autonomous*, but they have all agreed to establish some common institutions and to hand over some of their own decision-making powers to these international bodies. As a result, decisions on matters that interest all member states can be made democratically, accommodating everyone's concerns and interests.

Today, the EU is the most powerful regional organization in the world. It has evolved from a primarily economic organization to an increasingly political one. Besides promoting economic cooperation, the EU requires that its members uphold fundamental values of peace and **solidarity**, human dignity, freedom, and equality. Based on the principles of democracy and the rule of law, the EU respects the culture and organizations of member states.

History

The seeds of the EU were planted more than fifty years ago in a Europe reduced to smoking piles of rubble by two world wars. European nations suffered great financial difficulties in the postwar period. They were struggling to get back on their feet and realized that another war would cause further hardship. Knowing that internal conflict was hurting all of Europe, a drive began toward European cooperation.

France took the first historic step. On May 9, 1950 (now celebrated as Europe Day), Robert Schuman, the French foreign minister, proposed the coal and steel industries of France and West Germany be coordinated under a single supranational authority. The proposal, known as the Treaty of Paris, attracted four other countries—Belgium, Luxembourg, the Netherlands, and Italy—and resulted in the 1951 formation of the European Coal and Steel Community (ECSC). These six countries became the founding members of the EU.

In 1957, European cooperation took its next big leap. Under the Treaty of Rome, the European Economic Community (EEC) and the European Atomic Energy Community (EURATOM) were formed. Informally known as the Common Market, the EEC promoted joining the national economies into a single European economy. The 1965 Treaty of Brussels (more commonly referred to as the Merger Treaty) united these various treaty organizations under a single umbrella, the European Community (EC).

In 1992, the Maastricht Treaty (also known as the Treaty of the European Union) was signed in Maastricht, the Netherlands, signaling the birth of the EU as it stands today. **Ratified** the following year, the Maastricht Treaty provided for a central banking system, a common currency (the euro) to replace the national currencies, a legal definition of the EU, and a framework for expanding the

The EU's united economy has allowed it to become a worldwide financial power.

EU's political role, particularly in the area of foreign and security policy.

By 1993, the member countries completed their move toward a single market and agreed to participate in a larger common market, the European Economic Area, established in 1994.

The EU, headquartered in Brussels, Belgium, reached its current member strength in spurts. In

© BCE ECB EZB EKT EKP 2002

200

© BCE ECB EZB EKT EKP 2002

© BCE ECB EZB EKT EKP 2002

50

© BCE ECB EZB EKT EKP 2002

1973, Denmark, Ireland, and the United Kingdom joined the six founding members of the EC. They were followed by Greece in 1981, and Portugal and Spain in 1986. The 1990s saw the unification of the two Germanys, and as a result, East Germany entered the EU fold. Austria, Finland, and Sweden joined the EU in 1995, bringing the total number of member states to fifteen. In 2004, the EU nearly doubled its size when ten countries—Cyprus, the Czech Republic, Estonia, Hungary, Latvia, Lithuania, Malta, Poland, Slovakia, and Slovenia—became members.

THE EU FRAMEWORK

The EU's structure has often been compared to a "roof of a temple with three columns." As established by the Maastricht Treaty, this three-pillar framework encompasses all the policy areas—or pillars—of European cooperation. The three pillars of the EU are the European Community, the Common Foreign and Security Policy (CFSP), and Police and Judicial Co-operation in Criminal Matters.

QUICK FACTS: THE EUROPEAN UNION

Number of Member Countries: 25
Official Languages: 20—Czech, Danish, Dutch, English, Estonian, Finnish, French, German, Greek, Hungarian, Italian, Latvian, Lithuanian, Maltese, Polish, Portuguese, Slovak, Slovenian, Spanish, and Swedish; additional language for treaty purposes: Irish Gaelic.
Motto: In Varietate Concordia (United in Diversity)
European Council's President: Each member state takes a turn to lead the council's activities for 6 months.
European Commission's President: José Manuel Barroso (Portugal)
European Parliament's President: Josep Borrell (Spain)
Total Area: 1,502,966 square miles (3,892,685 sq. km.)
Population: 454,900,000
Population Density: 302.7 people/square mile (116.8 people/sq. km.)
GDP: €9.61.1012
Per Capita GDP: €21,125
Formation:
- Declared: February 7, 1992, with signing of the Maastricht Treaty
- Recognized: November 1, 1993, with the ratification of the Maastricht Treaty

Community Currency: Euro. Currently 12 of the 25 member states have adopted the euro as their currency.
Anthem: "Ode to Joy"
Flag: Blue background with 12 gold stars arranged in a circle
Official Day: Europe Day, May 9.

Source: europa.eu.int

Pillar One

The European Community pillar deals with economic, social, and environmental policies. It is a body consisting of the European Parliament, European Commission, European Court of Justice, Council of the European Union, and the European Courts of Auditors.

Pillar Two

The idea that the EU should speak with one voice in world affairs is as old as the European integration process itself. Toward this end, the Common Foreign and Security Policy (CFSP) was formed in 1993.

PILLAR THREE

The cooperation of EU member states in judicial and criminal matters ensures that its citizens enjoy the freedom to travel, work, and live securely and safely anywhere within the EU. The third pillar—Police and Judicial Co-operation in Criminal Matters—helps to protect EU citizens from international crime and to ensure equal access to justice and fundamental rights across the EU.

The flags of the EU's nations:

top row, left to right
Belgium, the Czech Republic, Denmark, Germany, Estonia, Greece

second row, left to right
Spain, France, Ireland, Italy, Cyprus, Latvia

third row, left to right
Lithuania, Luxembourg, Hungary, Malta, the Netherlands, Austria

bottom row, left to right
Poland, Portugal, Slovenia, Slovakia, Finland, Sweden, United Kingdom

ECONOMIC STATUS

As of May 2004, the EU had the largest economy in the world, followed closely by the United States. But even though the EU continues to enjoy a trade surplus, it faces the twin problems of high unemployment rates and **stagnancy**.

The 2004 addition of ten new member states is expected to boost economic growth. EU membership is likely to stimulate the economies of these relatively poor countries. In turn, their prosperity growth will be beneficial to the EU.

THE EURO

The EU's official currency is the euro, which came into circulation on January 1, 2002. The shift to the euro has been the largest monetary changeover in the world. Twelve countries—Belgium, Germany, Greece, Spain, France, Ireland, Italy, Luxembourg, the Netherlands, Finland, Portugal, and Austria—have adopted it as their currency.

SINGLE MARKET

Within the EU, laws of member states are harmonized and domestic policies are coordinated to create a larger, more-efficient single market.

The chief features of the EU's internal policy on the single market are:

- free trade of goods and services

- a common EU competition law that controls anticompetitive activities of companies and member states

- removal of internal border control and harmonization of external controls between member states

- freedom for citizens to live and work anywhere in the EU as long as they are not dependent on the state

- free movement of **capital** between member states

- harmonization of government regulations, corporation law, and trademark registration

- a single currency

- coordination of environmental policy

- a common agricultural policy and a common fisheries policy

- a common system of indirect taxation, the value-added tax (VAT), and common customs duties and **excise**

- funding for research

- funding for aid to disadvantaged regions

The EU's external policy on the single market specifies:

- a common external **tariff** and a common position in international trade negotiations

- funding of programs in other Eastern European countries and developing countries

COOPERATION AREAS

EU member states cooperate in other areas as well. Member states can vote in European Parliament elections. Intelligence sharing and cooperation in criminal matters are carried out through EUROPOL and the Schengen Information System.

The EU is working to develop common foreign and security policies. Many member states are resisting such a move, however, saying these are sensitive areas best left to individual member states. Arguing in favor of a common approach to security and foreign policy are countries like France and Germany, who insist that a safer and more secure Europe can only become a reality under the EU umbrella.

One of the EU's great achievements has been to create a boundary-free area within which people, goods, services, and money can move around freely; this ease of movement is sometimes called "the four freedoms." As the EU grows in size, so do the challenges facing it—and yet its fifty-year history has amply demonstrated the power of cooperation.

Europe is proud of its "bright idea," a union with economic and political power.

The EU believes that it can use its power to act as a "lighthouse" for the rest of the world.

Key EU Institutions

Five key institutions play a specific role in the EU.

The European Parliament

The European Parliament (EP) is the democratic voice of the people of Europe. Directly elected every five years, the Members of the European Parliament (MEPs) sit not in national **blocs** but in political groups representing the seven main political parties of the member states. Each group reflects the political ideology of the national parties to which its members belong. Some MEPs are not attached to any political group.

Council of the European Union

The Council of the European Union (formerly known as the Council of Ministers) is the main legislative and decision-making body in the EU. It brings together the nationally elected representatives of the member-state governments. One minister from each of the EU's member states attends council meetings. It is the forum in which government representatives can assert their interests and reach compromises. Increasingly, the Council of the European Union and the EP are acting together as colegislators in decision-making processes.

EUROPEAN COMMISSION

The European Commission does much of the day-to-day work of the EU. Politically independent, the commission represents the interests of the EU as a whole, rather than those of individual member states. It drafts proposals for new European laws, which it presents to the EP and the Council of the European Union. The European ssion makes sure EU decisions are implemented properly and supervises the way EU re spent. It also sees that everyone abides European treaties and European law. EU member-state governments choose the an Commission president, who is then ed by the EP. Member states, in consultah the incoming president, nominate the uropean Commission members, who must approved by the EP. The commission is appointed for a five-year term, but can be dismissed by the EP. Many members of its staff work in Brussels, Belgium.

COURT OF JUSTICE

Headquartered in Luxembourg, the Court of Justice of the European Communities consists of one independent judge from each EU country. This court ensures that the common rules decided in the EU are understood and followed uniformly by all the members. The Court of Justice settles disputes over how EU treaties and legislation are interpreted. If national courts are in doubt about how to apply EU rules, they must ask the Court of Justice. Individuals can also bring proceedings against EU institutions before the court.

COURT OF AUDITORS

EU funds must be used legally, economically, and for their intended purpose. The Court of Auditors, an independent EU institution located in Luxembourg, is responsible for overseeing how EU money is spent. In effect, these auditors help European taxpayers get better value for the money that has been channeled into the EU.

OTHER IMPORTANT BODIES

1. European Economic and Social Committee: expresses the opinions of organized civil society on economic and social issues

2. Committee of the Regions: expresses the opinions of regional and local authorities

CHAPTER SIX—THE FORMATION OF THE EUROPEAN UNION

3. European Central Bank: responsible for monetary policy and managing the euro

4. European Ombudsman: deals with citizens' complaints about mismanagement by any EU institution or body

5. European Investment Bank: helps achieve EU objectives by financing investment projects

Together with a number of agencies and other bodies completing the system, the EU's institutions have made it the most powerful organization in the world.

EU Member States

In order to become a member of the EU, a country must have a stable democracy that guarantees the rule of law, human rights, and protection of minorities. It must also have a functioning market economy as well as a civil service capable of applying and managing EU laws.

The EU provides substantial financial assistance and advice to help candidate countries prepare themselves for membership. As of October 2004, the EU has twenty-five member states. Bulgaria and Romania are likely to join in 2007, which would bring the EU's total population to nearly 500 million.

In December 2004, the EU decided to open negotiations with Turkey on its proposed membership. Turkey's possible entry into the EU has been fraught with controversy. Much of this controversy has centered on Turkey's human rights record and the divided island of Cyprus. If allowed to join the EU, Turkey would be its most-populous member state.

The 2004 expansion was the EU's most ambitious enlargement to date. Never before has the EU embraced so many new countries, grown so much in terms of area and population, or encompassed so many different histories and cultures. As the EU moves forward into the twenty-first century, it will undoubtedly continue to grow in both political and economic strength.

A small town in Austria

7 AUSTRIA IN THE EUROPEAN UNION

While not an original member of the EU, Austria has been working for years toward an integrated Europe. Finally, on January 1, 1995, the country was able to help accomplish this goal, and it joined the EU along with Sweden and Finland.

Economic Benefits

Once Austria joined the EU, it instantly became a more desirable trading partner to countries both in and out of the organization. Not only is it conveniently located between Eastern and Western Europe, but it is now a member of a common market and therefore more attractive due to the lowered trading tariffs.

Austria helped to found the Economic and Monetary Union (EMU), which is the organization responsible for the adoption of the euro as currency. Now that a common currency is in place, there is less risk of unfavorable exchange rates with the currencies of the country's other trading partners, such as the United States. In fact, a rising euro makes it worth more than the American dollar, giving members of the EU a trade advantage.

Gaining the Presidency

Every six months, a different EU country inherits the presidency of the organization. This allows that country to represent the EU's interests at international conferences. From July to December in 1998, Austria had its chance to be the mouth of this major organization. Because this role operates on a rotational basis, the country will get another turn in the beginning of 2006.

Skilled at Multitasking

Austria is a busy nation and is involved in all the various institutions and committees of the EU. The

One of Austria's mountain chalets

An Austrian newspaper kiosk

country takes an active role in such organizations as the European Court of Justice and the European Parliament, in which it holds twenty-one seats. It often holds sessions in the cities of Strasbourg and Brussels.

Austria is also involved in the Committee of Regions, which has 222 representatives from local governments. The representatives, including twelve from Austria, serve four-year terms and help decide such issues as the future path of the EU.

THE EU THREATENS TO EXPEL AUSTRIA

In 2000, the EU warned Austria that it had better be careful or it would find itself cut off from the rest of the organization. The reason for this threat? The rest of Europe was concerned about what would happen if the Freedom Party, a far-right radical group, were allowed to come into power. Austria was told that if it allowed the leader of this political party, Jörg Haider, to form a coalition with the less extreme conservatives, the EU would be forced to isolate Austria from the rest of Europe. This would mean that no EU government officials would have contact with their Austrian counterparts, the ambassadors from Austria would barely be tolerated, and Austrians attempting to apply for international government positions would find themselves without any support from the rest of Europe.

What was the EU's problem with Haider? He had expressed **xenophobic** views in the past. His outspoken respect of Hitler as a leader, along with the fact that he wanted to stop all immigration

Austria's flag

into Austria, combined to make the rest of Europe nervous about the results if he were allowed to rule the country, an outcome that seemed more and more likely as the Freedom Party got more than a quarter of the votes. Eventually, however, Haider was forced to resign, and Austria remained a member of the EU.

As the EU continues to gain strength and wealth in the years ahead, Austria will undoubtedly grow as well. As a result, the future looks bright for Austria.

A Calendar of Austrian Festivals

January: January 1 is **New Year's Day**. Epiphany is celebrated on January 2. Children dress up as the three wise men and travel from house to house bringing the news of Jesus's birth. They collect money for lesser-developed nations, but many people give them food as well. At Catholic homes, they will write an initial in chalk over the door, either C for Caspar, B for Balthasar, or M for Melchior (the three magi).

March/April: Easter is celebrated in either March or April. The Easter bunny comes and hides gifts in children's gardens. **Pentecost** is celebrated fifty days after Easter, and all of the schools are closed.

May: Labor Day is celebrated on May 1 with political parades and maypole dances.

June: Bonfires are lit on **Midsummer's Eve**, June 21.

October: October 26 is **Austrian National Day** (Nationalfeiertag). It celebrates the day in 1955 on which the neutrality acts were passed. It is also a fitness day when people exercise and all of parliament and museums are open for free.

November: All Saint's Day is celebrated November 1. It is a time to honor the dead and stems from the belief that the souls are among the living at that time. Food is given to the poor and to children. Young people may get gifts from their godparents. Bells ring, telling the souls that they are released and can leave the earth for another year. **Saint Martin's Day** (Martinstag) is November 11. Everyone eats roast goose. **Carnival** begins on this day—on the eleventh hour of the eleventh day of the eleventh month.

December: December 6 is **St. Nikolaus Day** (Nikolaustag). St. Nick goes and visits all the good children, putting presents in their shoes. On the other hand, Krampus will come and put coal in the shoes of bad children. Christmas markets also start around this time and will last throughout **Advent** until **Christmas Eve**. Christmas Eve is December 24. The Christ Child (Christkind) decorates the tree and brings the presents secretly that day. The presents will be opened that night. December 26 is **St. Stephan's Day (Boxing Day)**, the second day of Christmas.

Gebackene Apfelspaltan (Apple Fritters)

Makes about 24 fritters

Ingredients
1 cup flour
3/4 cup milk
1 egg
1 to 2 tablespoons sugar
3 medium apples
oil for deep frying
sugar and cinnamon (optional)

Directions
Mix the flour and milk together, and then add egg and sugar. Refrigerate batter for a few hours. When it's cool, blend again to get rid of any lumps that may remain. Peel and core the apples, then cut them into round slices that are about 1/4 of an inch thick. (Slice them so that a hole is left in the center where the core used to be.) Coat the apple slices in the batter, then fry them in 375°F oil until golden brown on both sides. Remove from the oil and drain on a paper towel. Dust with sugar and cinnamon if desired. Best served warm.

Erdäpfelsalat (Potato Salad)

Ingredients
2 pounds potatoes
1 red onion
2 tablespoons vinegar
4 tablespoons oil
salt
pepper

Directions
Cook the potatoes while they are still in their skins. Mix the other ingredients in a bowl, and then add the potatoes.

Topfenkolatsche (Cheese Danish)

Ingredients
Pastry:
1 package yeast
1/2 cup warm milk
1 3/4 cup flour
1/2 teaspoon salt
2 tablespoons sugar
1 egg
2 tablespoons melted butter
1 egg white
2 tablespoons chopped almonds

Filling:
2 tablespoons soft butter
8 ounces cream cheese
2 eggs separated)
1/2 cup sugar
grated peel of 1 lemon
1 tablespoon golden raisins

Directions
Pastry: Put the yeast in the warm milk, then sift
the flour and salt together into a warm bowl.
Add the sugar and stir in the yeast mixture. Beat
in the egg, then mix into a dough until it is
smooth and doesn't stick to the sides of the
bowl. Cover the bowl with a cloth and let rise
for about 1 1/2 hours. After it has risen, roll the
dough out into a rectangle that's about 1/2-inch
thick and cut into 3-inch squares. Arrange these
on a baking sheet.

Filling:
Combine the butter, cheese, egg yolks, sugar,
and lemon peel and beat together until the mixture is smooth. In a separate bowl, beat the egg
whites until stiff. Fold them into the mixture and
then add raisins.

Put about 1 tablespoon of the filling into
each dough square and fold the corners in
toward the center, pressing so the filling stays
in. Let the dough rise for about 45 minutes.
Brush the buns with egg whites and sprinkle
almonds on top. Bake at 400°F for 30 minutes,
or until browned.

Schonbrunnertorte
(a rich chocolate cake)

Ingredients
4 eggs (separated)
3 ounces sugar
3 ounces plain chocolate
9 tablespoons ground almonds

Filling:
3 ounces butter
3 ounces confectioners' sugar
3 ounces plain chocolate
1 egg
1/2 cup red currant jelly

Directions
Grind the chocolate and add the sugar and egg yolks, then the egg whites, and stir in the almonds. Put the mixture into a greased cake pan and bake in oven at 350°F 30 to 45 minutes, or until golden. Then cool.

Make crème by melting the chocolate and mixing it with the butter and sugar. After it is blended, add the egg and stir until it becomes foamy.

Cut the cake in half and spread the sides with the jelly, then with the crème. Put the sides back together and top with jelly and crème again. Decorate the top by drawing lines in it with a fork.

PROJECT AND REPORT IDEAS

Maps

- Draw a map of Austria showing its mountain ranges, rivers, highways, and major cities.
- Using papier-mâché, Play-Doh®, or flour and salt dough, make a map of Austria on a wooden board showing the mountains, rivers, and other geographical features.

Recipe for flour and salt dough:
4 cups flour
1 cup salt
1 1/2 cups hot water
2 teaspoons vegetable oil

Mix the salt and flour together, then gradually add the water until the dough becomes elastic. If your mixture turns out too sticky, simply add more flour. If it turns out too crumbly, simply add more water. Knead the dough until it's a good consistency. If you want colored dough, mix food coloring into the water before adding it to the dry ingredients. Or you can paint your creation after baking it at 200°F (93°C) for one hour.

Reports

- Write a well-researched paper on the history of the Roman Empire. Include in your report ways that the Romans influenced Austria's culture and nation.
- Write a biography of one of the famous musicians who lived in Austria.
- Write a report on anti-Semitism in Austria, and indicate the role that prejudice has played in many wars, including World War II.

Group Activities

- Divide into two groups for a discussion of the policies put into effect after World War II. One group should support the division of Austria carried out by the Allies, while the other group questions the fairness of this action.
- Role-play a discussion between a modern-day Austrian and one from the 1600s, when Austria was torn by rebellion and war. What differences would the two Austrians see in their nation? What similarities?

CHRONOLOGY

80,000–10,000 BCE	Austria is settled.
0	The Romans control the land that is now Austria.
700 CE	Charlemagne takes over the territory.
900s	Magyars from Hungary attack and conquer Austria.
955	Otto the Great vanquishes the Magyars.
1500s	The Ottoman Empire invades.
1600s	The Ottomans are defeated.
1618	The Protestants rebel against the Catholic Hapsburg emperor, leading to the Thirty Years' War.
1648	The Peace of Westphalia ends the war, making Austria a Roman Catholic nation.
1701–1714	Austria and France fight the War of Spanish Succession (Austria wins Belgium and Spain's Italian lands).
Late 1700s–1815	The Napoleonic Wars.
1815	Napoleon is defeated.
1859	Austria declares war on Sardinia and is defeated by Italy and France.
1867	The Austro-Hungarian Empire comes into being.
1914	Archduke Franz Ferdinand is assassinated and World War I starts.
November 3, 1918	World War I ends.
November 12, 1918	The last Hapsburg emperor is overthrown and the Austrian republic is formed.
1938	Hitler seizes control of Austria.
October 1939	World War II starts.
1945	The Allies defeat Germany.
1945	Austrian territory is divided between the United States, Britain, France, and the Soviet Union.
1954	The occupation of Austria ends.
January 1, 1955	Austria joins the EU.

FURTHER READING/INTERNET RESOURCES

Adams, Simon. *Eyewitness World War I.* New York: DK Publishing, 2004.

McDonough, Yona Zeldis. *Who Was Wolfgang Amadeus Mozart?* New York: Penguin Putnam Books for Young Readers, 2003.

Reef, Catherine. *Sigmund Freud: Pioneer of the Mind.* Boston, Mass.: Houghton Mifflin, 2001.

Roman, Eric. *Austria-Hungary and the Successor States: A Reference Guide from the Renaissance to the Present.* New York: Facts On File, 2003.

Stein, R. Conrad. *Austria.* New York: Scholastic Library Publishing, 2000.

Travel Information
www.aboutaustria.org
www.lonelyplanet.com/destinations/europe/austria

History and Geography
www.infoplease.com/ipa/A0107301.html
workmail.com/wfb2001/austria/austria_history_index.html

Culture and Festivals
www.austria-tourism.at
www.hudsoncity.net/culture/german/austriap.htm
www.wien.gv.at/english/culture.htm

Economic and Political Information
www.cia.gov/cia/publications/factbook/geos/au.html
www.photius.com/countries/austria/government/austria_government_government_andpolit~6617.html
www.wikipedia.org/wiki/austria

EU Information
europa.eu.int

Publisher's note:
The Web sites listed on this page were active at the time of publication. The publisher is not responsible for Web sites that have changed their addressees or discontinued operation since the date of publication. The publisher will review and update the Web-site list upon each reprint.

FOR MORE INFORMATION

Embassy of Austria
3524 International Court NW
Washington, DC 20008-3027
Tel.: 202-895-6700
Fax: 202-895-6750
e-mail: austrianembassy@washington.nu

Austrian Cultural Forum
11 East 52nd Street,
New York, NY 10022
Tel.: 212-319-5300
Fax: 212-644-8660
e-mail: desk@acfny.org

Embassy of the United States
Boltzmanngasse 16
A-1090 Vienna
Tel.: +43-1-31339-0
Fax: +43-1-310 06 82
e-mail: embassy@usembassy.at

European Union
Delegation of the European Commission to the United States
2300 M Street, NW
Washington DC 20037
Tel.: 202-862-9500
Fax: 202-429-1766

GLOSSARY

anarchy: Absence of any formal system of government.

anti-Semitism: Policies, views, or actions that harm or discriminate against Jewish people.

atrocities: Shockingly cruel acts of violence, especially during war.

autonomous: Able to act independently.

avant-garde: Artistically new, experimental, or unconventional.

baroque: A highly ornamental style of European art and architecture.

bisects: Divides into two exactly equal parts.

blocs: United groups of countries.

capital: Wealth in the form of money or property.

capitalist: Follower of an economic system based on private ownership of the means of production and distribution of goods, characterized by a free competitive market and the profit motive.

Celtic: Relating to someone who belonged to an ancient Indo-European people of pre-Roman time, who lived in central and western Europe.

coalition: The temporary union between two or more groups.

comparative advantage: When one country can produce something cheaper than another country.

constitution: The written document setting out the fundamental laws of a country.

currency: The bills and coins used as money in a particular country.

deciduous: Used to describe trees and shrubs that drop their leaves in the fall.

economies: Communities' production and consumption of goods and services.

erotic: Arousing, or designed to arouse, feelings of sexual desire.

excise: A type of tax on domestic goods.

fascism: A system of government characterized by dictatorship, centralized control of private enterprise, elimination of opposition, and extreme nationalism.

freedom of the press: The right of the press to report on matters without fear of reprisals.

gross domestic product (GDP): The total value of all goods and services produced within a country in a year.

hydroelectric: Relating to the generation of electricity by means of water pressure.

ibex: A wild mountain goat with long backward-curving horns.

income transfers: Government payments to individuals meeting certain criteria, such as low income.

marmot: A large, brownish, stout rodent of the squirrel family.

martin: A bird of the swallow genus with a notched or square tail.

militias: Armies composed of civilian soldiers.

nationalism: A strong sense of patriotism and loyalty for one's country.

opportunity costs: The added costs of using resources that is the difference between the actual value that results from those costs and that of an alternative use of those resources.

organic: Grown without artificial supplements or pesticides.

parliament: A house of government.

permeated: Entered something and spread throughout it completely.

police system: The use of the police, especially secret police, by a government to exercise strict control over a population.

precursor: Somebody or something that comes before, and is considered to lead to the development, of another person or thing.

privatize: To transfer state ownership of an economic enterprise or public utility into private ownership.

Protestant Revolution: A reaction to Catholicism characterized by the expansion of Protestantism.

provisional government: A government that is temporary or conditional, pending confirmation or validation.

radical: Favoring sweeping or extreme economic, political, or social changes.

ratified: Officially approved.

redundant: Repetitive, unnecessary.

reparations: Compensations for wrongs.

repression: The condition of having political, social, or cultural freedom controlled by force.

right: Political conservatism.

salt steppes: Vast, flat, and treeless tracts of land with salt deposits caused by evaporation of an inland sea.

secularization: The act of transferring something from a religious to a nonreligious use.

serfdom: The feudal European practice of having an agricultural worker cultivate land belonging to a landowner and who was bought and sold with the land.

socialist: A follower of the political theory or system in which the means of production and distribution are controlled by the people and operated according to fairness rather than market principles.

solidarity: Harmony of interests and responsibilities among individuals in a group.

stagnancy: A state of inactivity.

succession: The assumption of a position or title, the right to take it up, or the order in which it is taken up.

tariff: A tax levied by a government on goods, usually imports.

toleration: Official acceptance by a government of religious beliefs and practices that are different from the ones it holds.

totalitarian: Relating to a centralized government system in which a single party without opposition rules over political, economic, social, and cultural life.

vanquished: Defeated convincingly.

xenophobic: Having an intense fear or dislike of foreign people, their customs and culture.

INDEX

Picture Credits

Corel: pp. 10–11, 13, 16, 18–19, 26, 29, 30, 32–33, 35, 38–39, 40, 43, 44, 46–47, 49, 50, 66–67, 70

Used with permission of the European Community: pp. 52–53, 55, 58, 61, 62

Photos.com: pp. 15, 20, 36, 56, 64, 69, 72

To the best knowledge of the publisher, all other images are in the public domain. If any image has been inadvertently uncredited, please notify Harding House Publishing Service, Vestal, New York 13850, so that rectification can be made for future printings.

BIOGRAPHIES

AUTHOR

Jeanine Sanna lives in upstate New York with a variety of animals. In addition to being an author and journalist, she is interested in the field of forensic chemistry. Jeanine also enjoys traveling, music, and theater.

SERIES CONSULTANT

Ambassador John Bruton served as Irish Prime Minister from 1994 until 1997. As prime minister, he helped turn Ireland's economy into one of the fastest-growing in the world. He was also involved in the Northern Ireland Peace Process, which led to the 1998 Good Friday Agreement. During his tenure as Ireland's prime minister, he also presided over the European Union presidency in 1996 and helped finalize the Stability and Growth Pact, which governs management of the euro. Before being named the European Commission Head of Delegation in the United States, he was a member of the convention that drafted the European Constitution, signed October 29, 2004.

The European Commission Delegation to the United States represents the interests of the European Union as a whole, much as ambassadors represent their countries' interests to the U.S. government. Matters coming under European Commission authority are negotiated between the commission and the U.S. administration.